Letters to Kate
Claire Bankole

Letters to Kate

Published in the UK by Scripture Union,
207-209 Queensway, Bletchley, MK2 2EB, England.

Scripture Union is an international Christian charity working with churches in more
than 130 countries providing resources to bring the good news about Jesus Christ to children,
young people and families – and to encourage them to develop spiritually through the Bible
and prayer. As well as a network of volunteers, staff and associates who run holidays,
church-based events and school Christian groups, Scripture Union produces a wide range
of publications and supports those who use their resources through training programmes.

Email: info@scriptureunion.org.uk
Internet: www.scriptureunion.org.uk

Scripture Union Australia: Locked Bag 2, Central Coast Business Centre, NSW 2252
www.su.org.au

© Copyright Claire Bankole 2004
ISBN 1 84427 062 9

Other quotations are taken from *The Purpose Driven Life* by Rick Warren
(Zondervan); *What's So Amazing About Grace?* by Philip Yancey (Zondervan);
Journey of Desire by John Eldredge (Thomas Nelson); *Courageous Leadership* by
Bill Hybels (Zondervan).

British Library Cataloguing-in-Publication Data: a catalogue record for this book
is available from the British Library.

Photography and cover design by David Lund Design of Milton Keynes.

Internal design and typesetting by EH Graphics, East Sussex.

Printed and bound in Great Britain by Creative Print and Design (Wales), Ebbw Vale.

Letters to Kate

Claire Bankole

About the author

The first seven years of Claire's childhood were spent in Nigeria, her father's homeland, but it was at the age of 11 and after her parents had separated, at a mission meeting in London, UK, that she first met Jesus Christ and understood that he loved her. Later she trained as a doctor in Leicester, specialising in paediatrics. Though still only just into her 30s, Claire has worked with street kids in Guatemala, orphans in Mozambique, and some of the world's poorest people in south Sudan and north Peru with Tearfund and other relief organisations – all of which has been a transforming experience. She says, 'Everyone we meet in life, whatever status in society they hold, whether male or female, young or old, frail or strong – each one holds a unique treasure if we will only slow down and take the time to receive and, in turn, give them the priceless gifts we hold.'

Claire's passion is the church, particularly discipleship and community. As this book went to press, Claire was in Australia doing a youth and community course which she hopes will impact her ministry back in the UK.

Letters to Kate is dedicated to

Temi-Lola
*– may you always find your way to the Father's heart
and there discover a road less travelled by*

&

Mum & Katie Magill
– my heroes of the faith

Two paths diverged in a wood and I,
I took the one less travelled by,
And that has made all the difference.

From *The Road Not Taken*, Robert Frost

Dear reader,

As I reflect on how this book has come about and how I changed through writing it, I am thankful for God's faithfulness and that he would share his life with me.

Isn't it great to be part of a group of friends that love to share their journeys and their stories with one another? It can be so inspiring and encouraging for everyone concerned. In this collection of letters I have shared parts of my story and journey in the hope that you, the reader, would be encouraged and inspired on your own walk with God. It is my hope, too, that, as a result of reading, you would be challenged to think and talk through some of the issues that face us all as we try and live the 'life less ordinary' – the God-life.

Most of the story that unfolds in this book is true, but I have changed contexts and names to protect the identities of my friends. Once again I am reminded that I would not be the person I am if it weren't for God and the people in my life, so thank you to all those who have been friends for a season and to those who will be friends for life; thank you for walking with me and believing in me. In addition, thanks to Pete, Titi, Michael and Temi for loving and caring for me in the months after I got back from Sudan, during which time I finally sat down and wrote this book.

Claire Bankole

Year One

Following the God-life/ The lonely road/ Transition/ Temptation

September 20th

Kate! How are you? You'll never guess what happened to me today! I finally found a car! It's a 1977 left-hand drive Beetle – in baby pink!!! It is the coolest, sweetest thing I have seen in a long time. I knew God would come through on this one, but he has way upstaged all my hopes of 'something to pootle about in'! It's even got horsehair seats, would you believe, and that great 'old car' smell. You have to come and meet her for yourself; her name's Floyd – of course! She's great!

Anyway, let me settle down and get on with this letter. You asked me if I could write to you with some tips on how to survive moving to college, leaving behind the family home, church and everything you have known as you were growing up. You don't ask for much, do you!

And just one week to go!

There's so much that could be said in answer to all your questions … but after some thought I've come up with the four things that have really helped me find my feet over the years.

A month before I was offered the job in Sudan, I had a sense that Jesus was talking to me about how important it was in a dry country to dig cisterns or wells and to make sure that they were properly maintained. Looking back I realise that this was preparing me for both the spiritual and the natural aspects of my time there. Where we were in Sudan, the rains would start some time in June and the last rain would fall in November; after that not another drop would come until around the following June. It was crucial that enough rain fell during the wet season to maintain the water table at a high enough level to feed the one well we had. We also needed to ensure that the pump on the well was serviced regularly and not overworked, especially during the dry season. In that way it would last until the rains began.

> … blessed are those who trust in the Lord and have made the Lord their hope and confidence. They are like trees planted along a riverbank, with roots that reach deep into the water. Such trees are not bothered by the heat or worried by long months of drought. Their leaves stay green, and they go right on producing delicious fruit.
>
> *Jeremiah 17:7,8*

If water is a picture of what we need to keep spiritually healthy, rain could be all the external resources that God gives us for that – the church, Christian friends, worship, teaching etc. Our 'well', on the other hand, is our own relationship with God. Our direct, personal connection to him. Just as drought comes to the land in the natural world, so spiritually 'the rains' may fail at any time, so the 'well' needs to be kept in really good condition all the time.

As far as my heart and spirit were concerned, the time I spent in Sudan was a dry season with no rain. It was just me and God, pretty much. I sincerely believe that if I hadn't had the habit of setting aside time to spend with God in prayer, meeting him in his Word, journalling and worshipping him – spiritually, well, I would have died. I mean it.

As it was, those months were possibly some of the most significant in my life in terms of growing in my walk with Jesus and understanding more of his ways.

So that's my first tip. Make time on your own with God a habit. Let it be as routine as brushing your teeth! Do everything you can to keep these times alive – use Bible notes, journals, music, candles, painting – whatever!

My second tip is a bit like the first – make your walk through life with Jesus your number one priority in everything. Do everything you can to get to know him more. One thing I have started doing is to read through a gospel, one chapter a day. That's three months' worth of daily readings for you, if you go through all four gospels. It's a great way to get into the life of Jesus. The first time I did it, it impacted me in a big way. It brought to life and reality the man Jesus.

So, it's down to you to do all that you can to learn and grow as a disciple. Figure out how to approach everyday situations with God's perspective. Think about how to love like he does. Be salt and light.

> You are the salt of the earth. But what good is salt if it has lost its flavour?... It will be thrown out and trampled underfoot as worthless. You are the light of the world – like a city on a mountain, glowing in the night for all to see. Don't hide your light under a basket! Instead, put it on a stand and let it shine for all. In the same way, let your good deeds shine out for all to see, so that everyone will praise your heavenly Father.
> *Matthew 5:13-16*

There are loads of books out there that are really helpful. I'm sending you my copy of The Purpose Driven Life by Warren. Keep it – make notes in it, underline stuff as much as you want. Enjoy!

My third tip is to find a church as soon as you can. Since leaving uni I have moved city twice, and both moves were based on a church. I am not saying that's what you have to do, but that's how important I think it is. Sounds a bit extreme, but your relationship with God is the only relationship that will last through eternity. Being part of a Christian community is vital to growing in your walk with God. Find somewhere you feel safe and where you will receive good teaching either from the front or from mentors. And try to find some-where you can make good friendships, with people you can be accountable to.

By the way, get yourself grounded in relationships there before you fill your entire diary with church activities – I know you! One of the things I appreciated the most about being part of a church, especially during my first year in college, was having that window into the real life of real families and real people living it out in the real world… and home-cooked meals of course!

My fourth tip would be to keep in touch with people back home. OK, so you won't be able to do it with everyone, but I think it's important to keep an eye on your relationships with family and with two or three of your closest friends. Try to set aside time at least once a month or so to reply to letters and emails and return phone calls.

> Relationships, not achievement or the acquisition of things, are what matters most in life.
>
> *Rick Warren*

I think if you get one or two of these things sorted, you will do more than just survive the move to college. Stay close to Jesus, keep your heart soft to his voice and try to do what he asks of you.

Here's one of those handy quotes I keep on stuck on my fridge door. It goes like this: 'Sow a thought, reap an action; sow an action, reap a habit; sow a habit, reap a character; sow a character, reap a destiny'. It's a quote that helps me go back again and again to the habits that are shaping my life. I need to keep identifying the habits that need breaking as well as spotting the gaps that need filling. I always have some work to do!

Floyd and I are going on our first outing to the supermarket. The engine kind of roars in a loud but friendly car sort of way – they'll be able to hear us coming a mile off! I've got some of the guys coming round and thought I'd get the fondue set out again. I'm going to try and make the cheese one you did for our team end of term meal – that was so nice!

Listen, I hope the move goes really well and registration isn't too arduous. I'm sure you'll meet some nice people when you arrive. Will be praying for you.

God bless

Claire

February 4th

Dear Kate

    I was so chuffed to see your writing on one of the envelopes that dropped through my front door this morning ☺. It was great to hear from you, although I am sorry to hear that things are feeling a bit rough at the moment ☹. I remember my first weeks at college – everything is so new and there's so much to take in and adapt to. It often feels as if you are always the one who isn't quite sure where they are going and the last one to figure things out. Hang in there! It's just a matter of time before you feel right at home – you'll know all the short cuts, where to get the best coffee and cake, what times the buses with free seats come along, which librarian will willingly do searches for you and which bars and restaurants do student meal deals on which nights!

    It's hard being lonely. Entirely normal, extremely common – but still tough. One of the weird things I found being at college was that I was probably surrounded by more people than ever before and yet I felt incredibly isolated at times. Everyone has known that sense of being utterly alone in a crowd, like being in a bubble that's floating in a sea of people. But what is even worse is when you're in a room full of people you would call your friends and still you feel lonely – I hate that! You leave feeling somehow gutted, like you were expecting a slap-up three-course meal and all you got was a chunk of stale bread.

    Here's the thing… I reckon being alone and being

lonely are two very different things. And I've certainly found that you don't need to be alone to feel lonely. It seems to me that loneliness is a state of heart and it exists independently of your situation – whether you are on your own or with others. But if loneliness doesn't come from being alone then why does it happen and how do we deal with it? Obviously surrounding ourselves with lots of people and activity is not the answer, but we do our best to avoid the quietness of our own company and thoughts because that's when the loneliness buried within often finds its loudest voice. If being alone is supposed to be a positive and necessary part of our existence, we need to learn the secrets of experiencing it as a good thing.

> Instead of running away from our loneliness and trying to forget or deny it, we have to protect it and turn it into a fruitful solitude.
>
> *Henri Nouwen*

I can only tell you what I have learned and experienced and hope that it will be of help to you; at the end of the day the only infallible advice you will get is from God and his Word. What I know is that when I realised that being alone didn't mean that I was unloved, I didn't struggle with feelings of loneliness half as much as I used to – the state of my heart had begun to change and I no longer experienced solitude as a painful ordeal.

> … the Father … will give you another Counsellor, who will never leave you. He is the Holy Spirit, who leads into all truth.
>
> *John 14:16,17*

This was one of the most precious lessons I learnt when I was in Sudan. If you are in south Sudan, chances are you will be in a remote place. Our contacts with the outside world were through HF radio and the light aircraft that would come when the weather conditions were suitable. I was the only European in a team of five. And I was in charge! Sometimes I felt so incredibly alone that it was hard to do the simplest of things. I needed to know that God loved me, but I also needed to know that there were individuals in this world who also loved me and would do anything for me. We all need to be connected to someone; we all need to be in relationship.

My experience of loneliness usually boiled down to a fear that those connections had somehow been lost – that my existence was no longer of consequence and I didn't matter to anyone anymore.

Nowadays, if I sense those feelings beginning to take form again, I first try to take myself alone somewhere and reconnect with God – and then I reconnect with close friends. (That in itself has been a bit of a puzzle to me... the fact that being alone is, in fact, part of the answer to dealing with loneliness!)

> ... be sure of this: I am with you always,
> even to the end of the age.
> *Matthew 28:20*

Reconnecting with God is actually the easy part! He has placed his Spirit within us and wherever we find ourselves in this world he is right there with us. He said that he would never leave us or forsake us; one of Jesus' titles was the Good Shepherd and in the Old

Testament God was known as the Shepherd of Israel. In that culture shepherds lived close with their sheep to watch over and protect them, taking care of their every need. When we have responded to God's call on our lives and have begun walking with him, he has promised never to turn his back on us. We may turn away from him but he never turns away from us.

So we can come to him confident that he will be pleased to be with us. This is true even if we have done stuff that doesn't make him smile – because if we own up to it and ask him to forgive us, he will. End of story! Kate, you love Jesus and have been walking with him and doing his stuff for a while now – but don't ever forget the secret of keeping short accounts with him. Nothing is worth more than your relationship with Jesus, nothing is worth more than walking close by him through life. Remember, your relationship with him is the only one in which you will be able to receive untainted love, since he is the only being that is pure, holy and untainted by the world.

> … if we confess our sins to him, he is faithful and just to forgive us and to cleanse us from every wrong.
>
> *1 John 1:9*

Reconnecting with close friends can be a bit more tricky than reconnecting with God, not least of all because it can take years to form and build these friendships. Sometimes I just need to call up someone on the phone – maybe a friend, or perhaps my mum or a cousin. When I was in Sudan, I couldn't do that. It could take a few weeks between sending an email and receiving the reply, letters took even longer and there certainly weren't any phones!! To reconnect, I would look at photos, re-read letters and cards, or write to someone – all these things helped me as I remembered the people that cared for me. It was amazing to learn that I could be connected with someone and yet be hundreds of miles away from them; distance doesn't dilute the love of real friendship.

These days, since loneliness has become less of an issue for me, I have found being in my own company a completely new experience! Instead of being something to avoid at all costs it has become an important part of the balance in my life, crucial for getting to know God better and for understanding myself more. I have also grown to know who my close friends are and to have different expectations of those who aren't such close friends.

As you start off in college it will take time to build close friendships but you will find that a handful of them will remain friends for many years after you all disperse at the end of your courses – and surprisingly the people who end up being your lifelong friends often turn out not to be the ones you expected! The point is, while you are forming these friendships, you will need to stay connected with at least one or two of your really good friends from before college or members of your family.

Another thing: in the early months don't expect too much from your new friends. Friendships take a lot of work and it's hard to get the balance right between investing in new friendships and maintaining old ones. But, if you can do it, it will surely make for a rich and healthy existence!

My friend, this is all tough stuff, but it will make you stronger and you will be better equipped to deal with life. Some of the greatest people of faith in the Bible had some of their most significant training in isolation – David, Moses, Joseph, Jesus... God is preparing you for life his way. Be patient and stay connected to him; work at building new friendships and keep your old ones alive too.

> When you go through deep waters and great trouble, I will be with you. When you go through rivers of difficulty - you will not drown! ... you are precious to me ... I love you.
>
> *Isaiah 43:2,4*

Meanwhile, back here, the new term has started well. I am really excited about what God is going to do in and through the team. Liz is doing a great job with your girls – who incidentally are missing you like crazy! They were bubbling over on Friday about the notes and emails you had sent them last week. We do miss having you around here but it's so good to see you discovering the path that God has for you, even though it's hard at times. I am excited to see where it leads you.

Pink Floyd continues to be a roaring success, although I am looking forward to being past the worst of the cold weather as she is a tad draughty! My big news is that I'm picking up my puppy next week. I am sooooo excited – it's a bit of a dream come true, this one!

Well, let me know how things go. I am really pleased that you seem to have found a church to settle into already. It often takes a while. It is so important to have some connection with the 'real world' while at college. It would be great if you could find someone you can confide in there as well, someone you can go to for prayer if you need to. I'll pray that you do.

Anyway, Kate, keep in touch and don't forget that I am praying for you and thinking of you lots. And there are others praying for you and missing you as well. Jonathan and Kerry were asking after you the other afternoon.

All my love

Claire

PS How is your journalling going? Still thinking about this stuff about loneliness, the other day I remembered the story about Elijah. You know, after the Mount Carmel episode, Elijah felt really alone; he felt disconnected from God and from people. God's response was first to meet him in the still small voice that spoke to his heart. He made sure he had a nourishing meal and a good night's sleep – and then he gave him Elisha who would be his companion and someone to share with all that he knew of God. I found that really encouraging. God is so gentle with us.

And then there was Jesus in the garden of Gethsemane. He must have felt so dreadfully alone.

He got his closest friends to come with him, but they couldn't even stay awake – that must have been really hard to deal with, at one level. It kind of brought it home for me again that Jesus really does know what it's like to do life in this world.

If you ever get a chance to read Reaching Out by Henry Nouwen, it's a great book that deals with the issue of loneliness and solitude among other things.

June 23rd

Dear Kate

How are you? I am so glad that you have sorted who you will be living with next year. It can be a bit of a mission trying to work out which of your friendships will stand the test of living together. Have you been looking at houses yet or is it too early? How does it feel to have completed your first year? You must be looking forward to the summer break – make sure you plan in lots of fun and some rest! Jen and I have just booked train tickets for Scotland. I really hope Lucy behaves herself at the kennels. I shall miss her – but I am so ready for a break!

I have been thinking about what you said on the phone the other day. It can be really discouraging when we find ourselves struggling with the same things or patterns of behaviour over and over again;

stuff that we sincerely don't want to do but keep finding ourselves doing. Be encouraged, though, like I said. The fact that it's bothering you is a sure sign that God is doing his stuff in you and that you are growing.

> I know I am rotten through and through so far as my old sinful nature is concerned. No matter which way I turn, I can't make myself do right. I want to, but I can't. When I want to do good, I don't. And when I try not to do wrong, I do it anyway.
> *Romans 7:18,19*

The first thing to realise is that it is God who makes us Christlike – not us! The Bible says that it is God who works in us – we can't become like Jesus by sheer willpower! This way God gets all the glory himself and we can't get proud about how well we have done. All we have to do is to cooperate with God's work in our lives. We need to keep our hearts open to him, listening and hearing what he is saying to us and attending to the challenges he sets before us. This can be incredibly uncomfortable at times because he is totally committed to making us more like Jesus and he doesn't cut corners or sweep things under the carpet.

There are some things that I have found really helpful in dealing with stuff that comes my way and entices me to compromise my walk with Jesus. James explains in his NT letter that the root of sin and temptation is our own desires. Once I understood that enticement only really works if it relates to something that I want, it was easier to spot and easier to tackle. It's a bit like the rule of combat which teaches you to use your opponent's weight against him wherever possible; the devil discovers what the things are that we desire and basically entices us to fulfil those desires in ways that God did not intend or to a time plan that is different to (and often faster than!) God's.

> We think temptation lies around us, but God says it begins within us.
>
> *Rick Warren*

The other day I was with a good friend and a situation arose where I was strongly tempted to tell a 'white lie'; telling the lie felt like an easy way of keeping the friendship intact. For me the desire to be and feel connected to another human being is a really strong one so friendships are really important to me. Although I know that healthy friendships are built on trust, intimacy, truth and love, so that conflicts and difficulties can be dealt with openly and honestly, ultimately strengthening and deepening the friendship, I can be easily enticed to take all sorts of short cuts that will damage the friendship in the long run but give me a sense that I am maintaining 'contact' in that moment. Does that make sense?

Many of our desires aren't wrong or sinful in and of themselves but rather they are expressions of our humanness – that we are functioning the way that God created us to. Problems come, though, with the choices we make, when we let our desires drive us. So, although my desire to be connected with others is a reflection of God's image in me, if I let that desire drive me and I press on with what I want regardless of the consequences I could end up doing stuff that's unhelpful or just plain wrong. God doesn't intend for us to be ruled by our desires, he intends for us to learn to master our desires. It's easy to see how my desires are actually one of the devil's most powerful weapons against me!

> Temptation comes from the lure of our own evil desires.
>
> *James 1:14*

My journey in dealing with this sort of thing has meant first of all understanding what my desires are – just what are the things that drive me. And then I have to choose not to be controlled by them but rather to bring them to God and ask him to fulfil them in his own perfect way, in his own perfect timing. If I can trust God to answer the strongest, deepest desires in my heart then I am free to wait for him... I am free not to take those tempting short cuts... I am free to tell the truth to a friend even if the fear of hurting that connection is overwhelming.

There is one thing that's puzzled me on this journey I have been taking. I found that sometimes I think I want one thing when actually the underlying, real desire is for something similar yet different. You know what it's like when you want something, and you get it – but then you still feel dissatisfied? That's what I am talking about.

> We are half-hearted creatures, fooling about with drink and sex and ambition when infinite joy is offered us, like an ignorant child who wants to go on making mud pies in a slum because he cannot

imagine what is meant by the offer of a holiday at the sea.

C S Lewis

A great example is sex and physical intimacy. The desire for these can consume us however hard we try to control our thoughts and behaviour. Often we think that's what we want when actually what we are looking for is affection, or to be valued, to be in relationship, or just to be wanted and chosen. It is easy to see that sexual encounters won't come anywhere near to meeting any of those needs. What they will do, though, is bring us (and each person we sleep with) into conflict with God and his purposes for our lives, in particular in relation to sex and family life. His purpose is that an individual enjoys a sexual relationship with one person within the context of a lifelong marriage.

So one key to dealing with temptation is to check out your desires and see what it is you are actually looking for. Then bring those desires to God. If you can trust him with them you'll find the drive for physical connection at any cost will lessen – you will master it with his help and it won't be used to pull you out of relationship with God. Not that I'm saying this is easy – it's not!

Search me, O God, and know my heart; test me and know my thoughts. Point out anything in me that offends you, and lead me along the path of everlasting life.

Psalm 139:23,24

Yesterday I was with Naomi and I shared something with her that I had been struggling with and she was the first person I had ever told about it. As I shared, I noticed two things. First of all, the thing I had been struggling with seemed to shrink in significance and power. And secondly, I felt somehow free in a new way. I have asked Naomi to keep me accountable and to ask how I am going with this issue every now and then. Before speaking to her I felt totally overwhelmed by this thing. Now I feel empowered and free to deal with it responsibly. I would definitely encourage you to keep your struggles in the open with a trusted friend.

It's all about growing more and more like Jesus and learning to walk with him. It's about cooperating with him and living out what he has done and is doing in your life. The God-life is about God's work in us and us keeping in step with it. God delights in a heart that is surrendered to him and just longs to please him – you make him smile, Kate!

> … as the Spirit of the Lord works within us, we become more and more like him and reflect his glory even more.
> *2 Corinthians 3:18*

Be encouraged, keep going. It excites me to see you pressing into the life that God has called you to as his child. You're doing good – so hang in there!

With all my love

Claire

PS It would be great to spend some time catching up over the summer. Lucy and I had a lovely walk this afternoon. The cornfields outside the village are looking beautiful and the hedgerows are alive with wild flowers. Are you going to be in town the weekend after next? An old friend of mine, Alex, is staying over. I wanted him to meet some of the guys on the Saturday evening so we're having a meal at my place if you can come. It would be lovely to see you – there's space for you to stay over, too, if you want.

Postcard from Scotland

Hello you! Hope you're impressed I actually got round to writing postcards! It's wonderful up here – wide open spaces and not another soul for miles around. Breath-taking mountains and, oh, the sea here is young and wild! Lots more sheep than people – wouldn't Lucy just love that! We're sitting by a blazing fire, it's raining and blustery outside. I love it here! See you soon.
Claire

Year Two

Money and giving/ Priorities

To:	Kate
Subject:	re: small group discussion on money

Hey, Kate! Just dialled up and got your email. Here's a few short notes that might help as you prepare for Thursday night's discussion. I have to go out soon – I'm meeting Vicki for coffee in town (haven't spent any decent time with her for a while) and I need to do a few other bits and pieces while I am there. I'll have more time tomorrow to write longer but, for now, here's a few thoughts.

> Your identity is in eternity, and your homeland is heaven. When you grasp this truth, you will stop worrying about 'having it all' on earth.
>
> *Rick Warren*

I guess you'll need to think about tithing – New Testament and Old. it's an important one to get our heads around. Some issues that are good to raise are:
- tithing on loans (student loans?) – do you have to, since this is money that you don't actually own, but it is God's provision for you?
- what about mortgages?
- when you are in debt, is your priority to give and tithe or to pay off your debts?
- should those who earn tithe on the amount they get before they take away tax and national insurance or on what they actually take home?
- what about the whole thing of living on credit/credit cards and getting into debt?
- what are the ways we use our money that make God smile and what are the things we do with our money that cause him pain?

> ... he will give you all you need from day to day if you live for him and make the Kingdom of God your primary concern. So don't worry about tomorrow...
>
> *Matthew 6:33,34*

I guess this is all about how we run our lives; it's part of keeping our lifestyles in line with what we value and believe. Hmmm.

I'll think about it as I go through the day and write to you again in the morning when I have more time to give to it.

Good on you for taking this on!

Have a good one!

Claire

To: Kate

Subject: re: small group discussion on money

Hi Kate! How was yesterday? I had a good time with Vicki, we went to Café Noir (as usual!). She's doing well since her stay in hospital. She misses having you around to talk to, though she says you email a fair bit, which means a lot to her, and the group has settled down great with Liz who is doing a fantastic job. The time you used to spend with Vicki before you went to college, sharing your life with her, was precious and I don't think she'll forget it. She's adjusting to motherhood really well. It sounds like the whole family are doing well but we are going to have to make sure we are doing all we can to support them. Mavey being so cute and smiley helps a lot. It will be a challenge for Liz to navigate a girls' teen group with a mum and baby in it, but so far it seems to be going well. Anyway! Your discussion! The more I've thought about it the more I think what a challenging one it is for your first time leading in a new group! I'll be praying for you, my friend! It's great that you are getting involved, though. Just remember that God brought the individuals in your group together to learn and grow with each other which means that each person will have something to share and something to learn; your job is to make it a safe place for that to happen in a spirit of gentleness, truth and love. You don't have to make everyone believe a particular truth or practise a particular way of doing things! (relief hey?!) As I suggested yesterday, tithing is a good place to start when talking about the M word; it helps to raise issues of stewardship too. You could think about the following: some say we no longer have to be ruled by the OT laws because we have been brought into God's grace, BUT tithing started before the law when Abraham gave a tenth of his belongings to Melchizedek. Also: Jesus didn't come to abolish the law but to fulfil it...

> With Jesus' help, let us continually offer our sacrifice of praise to God by proclaiming the glory of his name. Don't forget to do good and to share what you have with those in need, for such sacrifices are very pleasing to God.
>
> *Hebrews 13:15,16*

The tithe was just one of numerous offerings that were required in the OT and I find it surprising, considering how much teaching there is on giving, that not a whole lot is said in the NT about tithing! You could get people to think about why there were so many different offerings in the OT and what God was saying to his people through them all – and then if and how that message changed with the arrival of Jesus.

Have you read Philip Yancey's book THE JESUS I NEVER KNEW? It's great, get hold of it if you can. One of the big take-home messages from the book is that if you actually sit and read the things that Jesus taught as if you had never heard them before, he was pretty harsh! He took the

OT law and raised the bar by several notches; no longer was it good enough to avoid having an affair with another man's wife, now you were guilty at the first lingering look you took. Jesus had this knack of somehow completely disregarding your actions but homing in on your heart; there was nowhere to hide.

I think the same happened with giving. No longer was it a matter of ticking the boxes, collecting 'points', obeying the rules. Now the priority was your heart, but there were also practical aims – (1) for the world to hear the good news of Jesus, (2) for the outcasts of society to be cared for and (3) that no one in the body of Christ should be in need. Sacrificial giving became the norm, it became intimate worship.

I think that Jesus' intention was for our giving to be a practical outworking of his command to love each other as he loved us. As we live this out, I reckon we will find that where there is a need in the body of Christ, somewhere there's also the answer.

> … all the believers met together constantly and shared everything they had. They sold their possessions and shared the proceeds with those in need. They … shared their meals with great joy and generosity.
>
> *Acts 2:44–46*

Here are some passages from the Bible that I've found helpful in thinking through some of this stuff on money and giving:

Luke 6:38; 12:13–21; 21:1–4

Acts 2:43–47; 4:32–37

If you have a copy of David Westlake's book UPWARDLY MOBILE, he has some really helpful insights into how the way we spend our money can care for others and make God happy, because often it does neither.

Look, I hope this is helpful for tomorrow. I would love to hear how it goes and to hear your own personal thoughts on this – how it all fits into your own life.

God bless

Claire

Sounds like you had a lively time! I guess it's a subject people find really challenging and so you can get some marked responses as peoples' buttons are being pressed! From what you say you handled it all very well, though.

> The more God gives you, the more responsible he expects you to be.
>
> *Rick Warren*

For me it's all about living in God's grace, acting out of obedience and love for him, not out of condemnation. The danger is that we are just as inclined to get into condemnation and strife over the issue of money as we are to rebel against what God is calling us to. The stuff I said about Jesus pushing up the standards for giving actually shifts the emphasis away from money itself, I think, and on to our own relationship with God and how we are doing with trusting him.

> The abundant life has nothing to do with material abundance, and faithfulness to God does not guarantee success in a career or even in ministry. Never focus on temporary crowns.
>
> *Rick Warren*

There was one time a couple of years back when I had more in the bank than I had ever had before. It just so happened that at the same time a good friend of mine from way back had run into some hard times. I had some ideas as to what I could do with the money but for various reasons my plans had to go on hold, so it didn't really make sense to me that he should go under while I had redundant money in the bank.

Giving him what he needed was still a brave step of faith … even though in one sense it didn't cost me anything, it meant letting go of security and trusting God again for my future. But I knew that this was how God had planned to meet his need. That's why I said that for me giving has become a lot more about my walk with Jesus and how much I actually trust him than about coins and notes. Besides, all I have belongs to him anyway. I am looking forward to seeing how he meets my needs as the future unfolds.

> He is no fool who gives what he cannot keep to gain what he cannot lose.
> *Martyred missionary Jim Elliot*

Now for an update on what's going on here!
The New Year has got off to a great start. The first 'festival' went really well at St Mary's High School and our guys are already coming up with some great ideas for the next one in March. I am so excited to see God building bridges between the church and the school community through the youth ministry from the kids to the caretakers, the parents to the governors. We are already beginning to see some of the fruit: a number of the parents are wanting to help run stuff next time, new kids are coming along to some of the regular youth meetings, relationships are forming and God is doing his stuff!! I wouldn't want to be doing anything else!
Go safely.
Love
Claire

Postcard from Devon

We arrived! Easter in Devon! Pink Floyd did good, though she did struggle a bit with the hills! But hey, we are having a wonderful time! Good food, good wine and great friends! The usual regime of gentle walks followed by cream teas – you can't beat it! I smiled when I saw the sea again, it's been a while! Lucy, Reuben and Missy are having a whale of a time – boy, they're a handful when they get together. Lots of love,

Claire

PS Happy Easter!

Year Three
Burnout/ Graduation/ Guidance

To:	Kate
Subject:	Bad day!

Hi there! Sounds like you are having some bad days over in your corner of the world! I have been praying for you as you asked. I just wanted to encourage you that you have done really well, even though it doesn't feel like it. You are on the last leg of the course, so hang in there! It won't be long before your finals are over and the pressure will be off. I'm sure you have days when you wonder if it's all worth it. Remind yourself of the reasons you started the course, the dreams you had at the beginning and know that you have got through so far – so there is no reason why you shouldn't be able to finish. God set you on this path, he has been with you up to now and I don't think he is going to leave you in the lurch at this, or any other, point.

> ... nothing can ever separate us from his love ... Our fears for today, our worries about tomorrow ... can't keep God's love away ... nothing in all creation will ever be able to separate us from the love of God...
> *Romans 8:38,39*

It does sound as if you are pretty run down, though. Try to look after yourself so that you can get through this last part of the course. I hope the doctor is helpful today. It may be an idea to book in to see one of the student counsellors at the surgery as well – they can be helpful when it comes to managing the stress of finals.
Be patient with yourself, my friend! You said you feel that you have let God down... you are getting squeezed and bad stuff keeps coming out! The worst part about when I got overstressed in my old job was that I could see myself turning into some kind of monster, and it felt like I had no control over it. I hated it because I could see that I wasn't

valuing and caring about people in the way that I wanted to. It made me realise that there is no way I can be the person that God wants me to be (and I want to be) without his help – masses of it and all the time. I had to learn to let God get on with what he loves to do – forming Christ in me.

> Human beings do not readily admit desperation. When they do, the kingdom of heaven draws near.
>
> *Philip Yancey*

So it's all part of the process; now you know just how much you depend on God to be the person you were made to be – you can't do that on your own. Meanwhile, do what you can to rebuild the bridges between you and your friends. You are all probably going through pretty similar stuff and it's my guess that you need each other more than ever right now, so try and make amends.
Let me know how you get on seeing the doctor.
Lots of love
Claire

To: Kate

Subject: re: re: Bad day!

Hi hon! Glad to hear the doctor was easy to talk to and you felt listened to. Sorry you are still feeling so rough, though. I have been thinking: you have been going at quite a fast pace for a pretty long time and it may be that your body has had enough. How would you say things are with you and God at the moment compared with maybe 3 months ago? I know things have been pretty rough with

your friendships lately. How are you finding being with people in general? Tell it as it is, Kate.
Lucy-Lou sends big doggy-love to you,
Claire

March 6th

Dear Kate

Hey you! Thanks for being so honest and open about how things have really been recently ☺. I did have my suspicions. It sounds like you are a bit burnt out ☹. From what you are describing, your emotions seem to have gone a little haywire, which is affecting your friendships, and you are not really able to cope with other people's lives. You and God aren't doing great and your body seems to be on its knees. Have I got that just about right? If I have, then some things probably could do with changing so that you can get through the rest of the year OK.

The freaky thing is that I have had to review my own life recently for very similar reasons. The youth ministry seems to be exploding. We've run five festivals with local schools over the past year and the fruit has been staggering. But I had got to the stage a couple of months back where I found I didn't care about the young people, and colleagues with difficulties were just another irritation in my day. I knew that something was badly wrong, that although I was doing what

God had called me to and made me for, I had somehow lost his heart along the way. I wasn't loving people anymore, and if I was honest I knew that in my heart I wasn't mad about God.

Here's something that Bill Hybels was told by some of his advisers who were concerned that he might be approaching burnout: 'The best gift you can give the people you lead … is a healthy, energised, fully surrendered (to Christ) and focused self. And no one can make that happen in your life except you. It is up to you to make the right choices so you can be at your best'.

That has stuck with me ever since I first heard it and I have been trying to apply the principles again to my life over the last month or two. Burning out doesn't do anyone any favours and it isn't the kind of sacrifice that God is looking for. He deserves our best, after all. I have started with the assumption that God won't ask me to do stuff without giving me all that I need to do it – including health and energy. So if I am in line with him I won't go too badly wrong. Trouble is, I am more inclined to live according to a rich cocktail of past experiences, guilt and expectations from all sorts of people – real or imaginary and including myself!

I have had to cut right back on the stuff that fills my days. I have had to review everything I spend my time and energy on and ask if it is what God wants me to be doing. If it is, it stays. If it isn't, it gets delegated or put on the back burner to wait God's timing. Now I am actually being obedient and I know that I can do everything he has given me to do – with

Jesus' help. Another little bit of wisdom: a successful businessman was asked what his secret to success was, his response was 'one thing'. Know what it is you are about and go for that 'one thing'.

In trying to sort my life out, I have paid attention to my body. I am being careful what I put in it and I am making sure I get plenty of fresh air, rest and gentle exercise. I remember when I was ill with Chronic Fatigue Syndrome a couple of summers ago, the doctors kept saying 'You must exercise!' But eventually I realised that your body can get to the place where normal exercise doesn't re-energise. Exercise for me then consisted of ten minutes walking each day – including around the house! Building up my stamina and strength was a much slower process than for an otherwise healthy person, but I still needed to work at doing it. You will have to listen to your body and gauge how much exercise is good for you right now and then work at doing that.

A new thing that I have done is to schedule time with God into my diary. I am planning to have a day retreat every couple of months. I am also meeting up with a couple from another church to chat and pray every couple of weeks and that has been amazing – so refreshing. It's great to know that there are others who are serious about standing with you as you try to live the God-life. I have realised, too, that I need to plan to hang out with like-minded people who will encourage me in my walk with God and keep me sharp in the things that I am doing. Basically I have decided that I have to be committed to keeping my love for God hot. I realise I had grown cold and stony

– and I don't want that to be my reality.

> Physical exercise has some value, but spiritual exercise is more important, for it promises a reward in both this life and the next.
>
> *1 Timothy 4:8*

I have also made new efforts to invest in my friendships, making sure I am spending time with good friends who genuinely love me. When I do that I feel so much better about myself!! It's about being kind to yourself. Doing creative stuff is something that has always done me good so I am making time for my music and art. Pamper yourself, watch some feelgood movies – you are probably quite vulnerable at the moment, though, so be careful what you feed your mind with.

Most things in my life fall into either the 'recharging' category or the 'giving out' category and what I am trying to do now is to make sure that each week there is a balance between the two. Looking back to the time before I made these changes, I can see that for a long period my time was badly unbalanced in this respect. I was doing very little that was recharging my batteries but loads that was giving out. I learnt that you can only keep that up for a short period of time. That's maybe what you are learning too.

Listen, I need to go to bed now, but let me know what you think about all this. If you want to chat through some of this stuff and how it applies to you, call me and I will call you back. Otherwise send a quick email.

God bless you loads. Be encouraged – he will help you through this time. Remember: it's not over till the fat lady sings!

Love

Claire

March 14th

Dear Kate,

Yeah, it's hard to work it all out. I am glad you have decided to take the doctor's advice and have a few days off to get properly well. What I would do when you go back is give yourself some practical guidelines to help you manage yourself so you're not overstretching all the time. For example, you could say that you won't have more than two late nights (past midnight) a week.

> ... Pursue a godly life, along with faith, love, perseverance, and gentleness.
>
> *1 Timothy 6:11*

And don't forget, Jesus spent whole nights on his own with the Father. The gospel writers made a point of telling us when he did this before and after great events. He did not assume that he could go on doing his stuff without taking time out to receive from his Father. Look at the things you are involved in, the relationships in which you give out, and make sure that your private life with God is sufficient to sustain that level of output. If it isn't, cut down on the things you are involved in and do what you need to do to improve your private walk with Jesus. With time you may be able to crank up your output again.

It may sound a bit pious, but for me it's been about ordering my life in such a way that I make God smile because my priority is to serve his purposes and to live effectively for him. For you, right now, that means getting through your course with minimal damage to yourself and your relationships both with God and with others. I know that there will be times when God puts me in situations where I have to give out more than I am receiving (finals week is going to be one of those times for you) but they won't last forever and if I have been careful to be balanced beforehand there will be enough reserve to meet the new requirements.

> … do not let yourself be tied up in the affairs of this life, for then you cannot satisfy the one who has enlisted you in his army.
>
> *2 Timothy 2:4*

Sometimes God makes us find new ways of recharging by changing the situation we find ourselves in – this, too, is part of growing us and equipping us for the road ahead. Long-distance runners pace themselves so that they have enough reserve at the end of the race to sprint for the finishing line. But no long-distance runner would think of sprinting for the whole race. It's the same with life – we need to walk slow and steady but always be ready to run. Part of being ready is making sure that your reserves are full.

You've just got to do what you've got to do!

I know from the experience of the last couple of months that it is hard to make these kinds of extensive lifestyle changes, but I don't honestly think there are any short cuts available to us. So grab the bull by the horns and go for it. Why not let's keep each other accountable on this? I am concerned that you get over this illness properly so that you can concentrate on getting through the next few months until your finals. I am going to put a couple of recipes in the post to you – cheap, healthy eating. Hope you like them!

Let me know if there is anything that I can do to help.

God bless

Claire

PS I am finally facing the fact that Pink Floyd's days as my primary means of transport are probably over. She has served me well but sadly I feel we are coming to the end of an era! I need a newer, more reliable car!

To: Kate

Subject: Food for thought!

Hi!
Just a quick email. Turn your thoughts to this meditation, it really is going to bless you! I'm sure I've mentioned this to you before, but there's just so much here that's really so appropriate for you right now.
1 Kings 19: Elijah had just given out spiritually, emotionally, mentally and physically – to the max! He had defeated Baal's prophets and had them all executed. He had laboured in prayer, bringing an end to a 3-year drought. He had outrun a horse-drawn carriage. He had led the nation and their king. Then he reached the end of himself and went on the run alone and dejected – like a hunted animal.
Then God, the loving, gracious Father and Shepherd gave him physical rest, food and water. He met Elijah in a deeply intimate and personal way. He gave him a strategy and plan to think on and implement. And finally he gave him a companion for the road.
Here are some other passages that have inspired me as I have been re-ordering my life:
Isaiah 40:27–31
I Timothy 4:7,8,16
2 Timothy 2:3–7
Love
Claire

Get well card

Dear Kate,

Here's to a complete recovery in good time. Rest
well and get well. Hope you are soon well enough to
cook this...

Gently fry half a chopped onion, one chopped sweet
pepper, a crushed clove of garlic and a pinch of cumin
seeds in a tiny bit of oil. Once the onion and green
peppers are tender add some chopped courgettes (or
parsnip or sweet or normal potato – these would need
to be cut small and partially cooked in boiling water
for a couple of minutes beforehand). Stir for a few
minutes then add some passata or a tin of tomatoes
and simmer gently, adding a tin of chick peas (or other
cooked pulses or lentils), a teaspoonful each of paprika
and coriander and half a teaspoonful of powdered
cumin and a small pinch of chilli pepper (crushed or
powdered) and some salt. Simmer for 5 minutes and
serve with rice, pasta or couscous, with fresh coriander
to garnish if you are feeling posh!

Praying for you
Claire and Lucy-Lou

May 20th

Dear Kate

It was so great to see you the other evening. I love visiting you where you are, reminding myself of your surroundings. You look so much better than earlier on in the year. Well done for having the courage to make the changes you did – I wouldn't be surprised if some of them have set you up now to be able to really go the distance. It's a tricky time for you at the moment, coming up to your finals while all the time at the back of your mind is that looming question of 'what next?' Hang in there! From what you were saying over dinner there isn't anything you can really do at the moment – future plans-wise – so try and give yourself permission to concentrate on your exams and think about the future afterwards.

> '… I know the plans I have for you,' says the Lord. 'They are plans for good and not for disaster, to give you a future and a hope.'
> *Jeremiah 29:11*

From where I stand, God has led you clearly till now and he's not going to take a break from doing so! He is also quite capable of letting you know what he wants you to do.

Whenever I've come to a crossroads in my life, (something that seems to happen with monotonous regularity!) I've found it's important to look for certain things when I am trying to work out what God is wanting me to do.

A major, major way of God talking to us and guiding is, of course, the Bible. As I spend time on my own with him he leads me, prompts me and guides my thoughts. Then, he'll tweak my circumstances or just let me see them in a new light. Before, after, or at the same time I'll find he's confirming all this through the Bible, through the words of a stranger, or a friend who has been praying for me.

> … the word of God is full of living power. It is sharper than the sharpest knife, cutting deep into our innermost thoughts and desires. It exposes us for what we really are.
>
> *Hebrews 4:12*

(I remember years ago when I was at uni we had a visiting speaker who was teaching on prophecy and he said when God speaks to us through another person, he's usually confirming what he's already said to us in private. I've found that really helpful in knowing how to respond to what people say.)

The Bible, my own time with God, my circumstances, something someone else says: when all these things come together I know it's just a matter of time before things begin to click into place!

The other big thing that I rely heavily on to know what God is wanting for my life is his peace. I have been trying to learn how to let God's peace rule my heart and mind and so lead me. As soon as I realise I've lost it (God's peace, I mean!), I know I have to trace my steps back to where I last had it and, with God, revisit the decisions I've made since then till I get it back. I try not to go anywhere knowingly without the peace of God.

> ... Tell God what you need, and thank him for all he has done. If you do this, you will experience God's peace, which is far more wonderful than the human mind can understand. His peace will guard your hearts and minds as you live in Christ Jesus.
>
> *Philippians 4:6,7*

I remember when I was making the decision whether or not to go to Sudan, I knew I would be stretched beyond what I had ever experienced before; I knew it would be dangerous. I was nervous and excited but, despite all that, I had this amazing sense of God's peace about the whole thing. And then a few months later I got sick and I was in Nairobi trying to figure out whether to go back into the Sudan or not. My colleagues wanted me to go back, it seemed the sensible thing to do just for a week to tie up some loose ends but the truth is while I was considering that option God's peace had left – gone, it was nowhere in sight! The moment I decided and asserted that I wasn't going back, it returned. I'll never forget that! God has a way of leading us even when we face the most tricky dilemmas.

> The Lord says, 'I will guide you along the best pathway for your life. I will advise you and watch over you.'
>
> *Psalm 32:8*

And if in doubt, check it out against what God has shown of his heart in the Bible. It's great to know – and easy to forget, I find – that Jesus does actually want to share his thoughts and plans with us and he loves to do so in the context of a genuine friendship with us. The thing is, we need to spend time nurturing that friendship by being with him and talking with him.

One of the things I used to struggle with a lot was how to hear God's voice. I seemed to be surrounded by people who appeared to hear God speaking pretty clearly, almost audibly, practically on a daily basis, and that freaked me out because I didn't!

> If you need wisdom – if you want to know what God wants you to do – ask him, and he will gladly tell you... But when you ask him, be sure that you really expect him to answer …
>
> *James 1:5,6*

Then Jesus showed me that he had made each of us completely different (duh!) but one of the differences that he specially delights in is the way each of us connects with him and converses with him. I tend to connect with God very much with my heart, at a gut level, and I will often get a sense for what he is saying a long time before I can express it with words.

The relief when I realised that, not only was that OK but also that God delighted in it, was fantastic! It's about learning what the languages are that God has placed in you to relate to him and then using them to listen. When you start to think about the possibilities, it's incredible. He can use all our senses to communicate with us: sight, sound, smell, hearing, touch; our body; our intellect and mind; our heart and emotions; our spirit; our character; our personality; our environment; our background – its endless! Who knows what he wants to say to you? There's only one way to find out!

Another thing that's really important in working out what God's saying, especially directional stuff, is having trusted friends who are looking out for you and praying for you and to whom you are accountable. It's good to have more than one person who you can call and sound out about stuff; people who you know have your best interests at heart. The people in my life who have known me the longest and remained faithful friends and open to God's heart for me are the ones whose opinion I value most highly. New friends and leaders can also bring fresh perspective and often confirm old callings, which can be hugely encouraging! You can also have people mentoring you in specific areas that you want to grow in. I remember the time a few years ago when I had a youth work coach (when I was coordinating the youth work at church), a worship mentor (I wanted to develop my skills as a worship leader) and a general mentor, as well as old-time friends who I held myself accountable to! I grew so much during that time with all that input and feedback, it was phenomenal!

> The heartfelt counsel of a friend is as sweet as perfume and incense.
>
> *Proverbs 27:9*

So I'd really recommend you to try to gather these kinds of people around you, and ask them to take some responsibility in seeking God with you; it's good practice, it's healthy. But a word of caution – it's not always straightforward! In my experience, sometimes personal stuff can get in the way. Even the most devoted mentor can have his or her own agenda and we all fall into the trap of trying to make things work out the way we think God wants them. Don't despair though, it is worth it! Just remember to stay with the Bible and with the peace of God and you won't go too far wrong.

I am a bit of a 'can do' person but that means that I find it difficult sometimes not to try and make things happen. People like me need to learn how to wait! When God's time comes for something to happen, the most outrageous, miraculous things can occur with almost no effort at all. It's like the difference between having to kick the front door of your house down because you lost the key and finding it just ajar and all it takes is the lightest push to get inside. Superb! But still, it's hard to wait sometimes.

> Don't be impatient for the Lord to act!
> Travel steadily along his path...
> *Psalms 37:34*

One of the things that I realised not so long ago is that God's timing has very little to do with a watch and a calendar and a lot to do with the hearts of his children. I am beginning to see that what happens to any one of us will automatically affect hundreds of other people now and for eternity – and I think Jesus often chooses to wait for a number of hearts to be in a certain place before he sets things in motion for any one of his followers. We really are part of his bigger purpose!

I'll be praying for you, Kate. Concentrate on your finals for now. I know that your heart is leaning towards serving God's purposes in your life and that is not a small thing to him. When the time is right he will let you know what it is you are to do. Plus he will make sure you hear and understand and he will make the way ahead clear to you – all in his time. For now you have a degree to complete.

> ... the Lord has already told you what is good, and this is what he requires: to do what is right, to love mercy, and to walk humbly with your God.
>
> *Micah 6:8*

Thanks for the treats you got for Lucy ☺. You're not the only one looking forward to 'after finals' when you can come down and go for long walks with her in the country!

With all my love

Claire

Graduation card

Congratulations on your graduation, you made it!!!! Well done! Well done for all your hard work. Well done for sticking with it even when your health problems were stacked against you. Well done for not being afraid to grow over the past three years. Well done for persevering with the God-life even when it seemed hard and tedious. I am excited to see what happens as you discover what God has for you – the story he has for you to tell with your life that echoes the song that he sings over you and you only!

God bless you, my friend,

Claire

Year Four

Blessings and hardships/ Authority/ Conflict

September 25th

Dear Kate

How are you? Just been reflecting on the past few months and the journey you have taken; how God opened the door for you to go to Peru. Isn't it amazing! You were an inspiration to me in the way you remained peaceful and confident that God would make a way once you had a sense of what he wanted you to do. And here you are in the centre of an unfolding plan. Great to get your first news from 'deepest darkest' and to hear your journey went off without too many problems. My most memorable journey ever actually happened in Peru. It was the internal flight I had in Peru from Lima to Moyobamba when I got off the plane at the wrong airstrip. Thank God I relaxed enough to let the luggage boy talk to me and so found out that the reason my cases had not yet surfaced was that this indeed was not Moyobamba but Tarrapoto!! A moment later I was running across the airstrip to the plane which was already repositioning for takeoff. One of life's more embarrassing moments!

Thanks for your letter. It's really made me think again about the spectrum of lifestyles, experiences, blessings and suffering that we see as we walk through the world; how do we make sense of that, what is the God-reality of it all? It seems the full range is part of life whether you are a Christian or not, and bad things still happen to good people. When we travel to other parts of the world, it's like our eyes are opened because of the newness of our surroundings, and somehow the contrasts seem starker than at home. The gap between the 'haves' and the 'have-nots', between those who are blessed and those who are not, seems to be somehow wider. I have found myself looking desperately for rhyme or reason, cause and effect, but each time I come back to the question: what does it mean to be blessed by God?

> ... If any of you wants to be my follower, you must put aside your selfish ambition, shoulder your cross daily, and follow me. If you try to keep your life for yourself, you will lose it. But if you give up your life for me, you will find true life.
>
> *Luke 9:23,24*

Isn't it interesting that in the midst of the most scandalous of hard times which God himself seems to allow, Jesus meets us with kindness and love? How does that work? I don't know. I saw it in Mozambique during those floods as I made my way from the villages to the orphanage, from the city slums to the supermarket. Again, in Guatemala working with the street kids in the middle of the city, and in south Sudan with some of the world's most desolate and poor... What does it mean to be poor? What does it mean to be blessed by God?

Sometimes I find myself feeling guilty when I see what I have in comparison to what others have. I somehow feel that I'm not genuine because I'm not destitute. At those times I have learnt that I need to make sure that my motivation to serve others is not guilt but love. We are called to a life of love not of guilt.

Other times, I find myself wondering what I have done to cause the hard times that have come to me! At those times I need to have the courage to trust in God's grace and his ability to save and I need to keep on living the God-life despite what happens.

> ... I have learned the secret of living in every situation, whether it is with a full stomach or empty, with plenty or little. For I can do everything with the help of Christ...
> *Philippians 4:12,13*

The late John Wimber used to say that we are all just loose change in God's pocket. I guess that's the point – God is God and he can do what he wants. We are his. We exist for his purposes, not for our own. Life and all that goes on around us is about God working out his purposes for humanity. I used to think life was all about me. That's even how I viewed God's call on my life – essentially it was about finding out what would make me happy and fulfilled, then doing it. How pathetically wrong I was! Being obedient to God and walking with Jesus has meant doing the most frustrating jobs with difficult people and going way into the red on my health, energy and emotional 'accounts'. Others lose their jobs, their loved ones, their freedom. Outrageous numbers still lose their lives – all because they choose to walk with Jesus; they choose to be obedient to his call and purposes for their lives.

For me that's still not the full picture though. Not only are we loose change in God's pocket but, at the same, time we are the apple of his eye. It's like you have to grab hold of one aspect of God without letting go of another even when the two seem to contradict. None of the hard stuff that happens to us or anyone else is grounds to think that he loves us any less than infinitely. Because of his love he chose to die for you rather than live without you. This is what I call the impertinent truth of God's love for us and we need to know it in the depths of who we are.

It dawned on me this morning as I was being quiet before the day started that Jesus knew God's love and favour to extents that are beyond our understanding, and yet his love for the Father and for us led him to live a life stripped of his rights and privileges as God, and ultimately it led him to extreme suffering and death. I have a feeling that somewhere in that tale is hidden the answer to what it means to be poor and what it means to be blessed and favoured by God. This is the life he has called us to live and I am wondering if, as we do so, we will be able to see a bit more of God's perspective on some of this stuff.

> Your attitude should be the same that Christ Jesus had. Though he was God, he did not demand and cling to his rights as God. He made himself nothing; he took the humble position of a slave and appeared in human form. And in human form he obediently humbled himself even further by dying a criminal's death on a cross.
>
> *Philippians 2:5-8*

Thank you for making me revisit this. I would love to know if what I have said makes sense in your own context in Peru. I hope you enjoy the tapes I sent you of the last couple of Sunday morning services at church.

Let me know if there is anything you would really like. Are you getting lots of teaching? Do you need more in the way of new music stuff? Just let me know, hon.

Great news! We have reached a significant point with the festival programme. Having grown it up from the start, the events side is now being run by a team of people led by Jon and all I have to do for the next festival is turn up on the day and celebrate their hard work and vision. Phew! It's so good to be in on what God's doing! We have run three Alpha courses for people we've got to know through the festivals, and the schools work has mushroomed!

Whenever I think of you out there I get excited about the year ahead of you and wonder what adventures God has in store for you; it's going to be a really significant year for you, I am sure!

God bless you, my friend.

With all my love

Claire

Hi! How are you?? Thought I'd wiz a quick 'hello' to you out in 'deepest darkest'.

It's been great getting all your updates as you've been settling into life in Peru. A bit different to college life, hey? You seem to be navigating all the challenges with deft ability, though. Glad that you get on with your room mate so well. How are you adjusting to the food and climate? Have you had guinea pig to eat yet?

Got a few scraps of news to keep you going for the day: I just got off the phone to Alex and he sends you his love. He is doing well, crazy as ever – has just embarked on yet another one of his business ventures with an old friend as his partner. No doubt it will be as eventful an escapade as everything he does usually is.

Mavey was 2 on Friday! (Can you believe it?) Vicki put on a birthday party for her at the village hall on Saturday afternoon. It was wonderful! There were about 25 kids there, some from church, some from her village, and a fantastic assortment of parents. In true Vicki style she had put huge amounts of effort and thought into the afternoon. There were loads of games and activities and she had even done separate food spreads for the adults and kids, it was amazing! Andy and Naomi were helping out, too. You should have seen Mavey's face when the cake was brought in and everyone started singing... I'll send you the pictures when they come through. I had a nice chat with Vicki's mum while we were clearing up in the kitchen. She's great, isn't she!

I loved your story about the little boy and the puppets you made. So much of what we take for granted as normal comes across as plain insanity to others around the world! But I am glad that the crafts are going well and the puppet

stand came good.
Watch out for stray teddy bears...
Lots of love
Claire

PS how are things going with your director? I remember you were a little concerned about how it was going to be, working with him...

To: Kate

Subject: re: me and the boss

Ah! So that's how things are! Be careful how you handle this one. It could be a really positive thing for your growth or it could ruin the rest of your stay there, depending on how you tackle it. No pressure, you understand!
You are a wonderfully passionate, energetic lady with huge potential and gifts in leadership which Jesus will use throughout your life. You will find your gifts and skills being stretched and strengthened at every turn. I know it's hard, but some of the best training for leadership comes through learning how to be led. There are many leadership styles and every leader is at a different stage of development in their gift; and not surprisingly it can be difficult to be led by someone who doesn't do things the way you would.
Submitting to another person's authority and leadership is one of the most important lessons in life to learn – and really equips you to become a leader! In my experience, in whatever situation I find myself, the amount of authority I

have and its degree of effectiveness seems to be directly proportional to the extent to which I am myself under authority; and I cannot be an effective leader without authority. Effective, authentic authority is always given and never taken.

> ... all of you, serve each other in humility, for God sets himself against the proud, but he shows favour to the humble.
>
> *1 Peter 5:5*

When I first started doing the youth work at church we brought in a lot of changes and I could not have done that without Dave's backing. Being submitted to him, making sure he was OK with everything that I was introducing and doing, meant that I had his authority behind me and if anything went wrong – which it sometimes did – he was ready to back me up.

Do you remember in the gospels when Jesus is met on the road by a Roman officer who asks him just to speak the word so that his servant will be healed? He believed that because Jesus had been sent by God the Father, he therefore had authority over sickness since he was on a mission from God who had authority over everything. His understanding of the identity of Jesus was nearly as profound as Peter's when he said that Jesus was the Messiah – that's why Jesus was so impressed.

If you can get your head around this issue you will save yourself a lot of heartache down the road. Submission gets a lot of bad press these days but it is so good! Not only does it authenticate your authority and leadership, making your life and job so much easier, but it also offers you protection. Also because you are obeying God by submitting to your leaders, God himself will honour you – isn't that amazing! You submit and suddenly you're backed by not just those over you, but all of heaven too. When it comes down to it, it's not so much a matter of honouring your leaders as it is of honouring God who takes note of those who trust him and obey him.

Here's another thing to consider: the more your director sees you are trustworthy within the project, the more he will be inclined to trust you. Being patient with the restrictions he is placing around you now could mean that in a couple of months you find yourself being released more. As Dave became more confident in me as a leader, all he wanted was for me to give him regular updates rather than running everything by him before taking action – but it took time for that to happen.

> Be sure to do what you should, for then you will enjoy the personal satisfaction of having done your work well, and you won't need to compare yourself to anyone else. For we are each responsible for our own conduct.
>
> *Galatians 6:4,5*

Does all this make sense? How does it change your perspective on things?
Let me know how you get on with all this.
Love
Claire

To: Kate

Subject: re: re: me and the boss

Thanks for that Kate, you've made me think! I guess it's a matter of being true to ourselves and accountable to God for our own actions; submitting to leadership is not to be at the expense of our own integrity, it is part of the God-life, not in contradiction to it. You are allowed and expected to use your discretion; I would encourage you to be upfront about everything. At the same time, though, we need to learn to value the integrity of our leaders. We may not appreciate or fully agree with their convictions but they have to give an account before God. If you genuinely believed something to be right or God's preferred way of doing things, the only way you could come before God each day with a clear conscience on the subject was if you were to hold firm to your belief and act accordingly.

It may be that that is just what your boss is doing and it may be, too, that God honours him for that. I used to get really frustrated with some of the rules that Phil had. They flew in the face of what I felt I was supposed to be doing for God. But I know that God had me there for a purpose, part of which was to learn grace and submission and to trust God to accomplish his purposes for my life.

> Love each other with genuine affection,
> and take delight in honouring each other.
> *Romans 12:10*

So, I guess that's it. Trust God with this one. Keep your heart soft. Take your frustrations to Jesus. Be patient, my friend.

Kate, this is going to be one of the most uncomfortable issues you have had to address, so be patient with yourself. It was probably easier for you being on the youth team since we all got on and knew each other well; it's harder to 'humble out' with people you don't necessarily get on or agree with. I really do think the way you deal with this will shape the path ahead of you in a big way, but having said that I don't underestimate how hard it is.

I will be praying for you! I pray too for the puppet boy and all the others like him with whom you are sharing your life at the moment. May God bless you all by making his loving presence tangible in countless ways over the coming months.

Keep me posted.

With all my love

Claire

PS I was journalling about this stuff the other night and it occurred to me that Jesus submitted to God the Father ... Mary and Joseph ... the Roman authorities ... and the religious leaders; and he never once compromised his identity as the Son of God. Isn't that amazing? I am still working on how to live this stuff out in every area of my life...

Here are some passages that I found; they are really challenging:
1 Samuel 24:1–22
Romans 13:1–7
1 Timothy 2:1,2
John 19:11
Hebrews 13:17

A couple of books I have which are really good on this subject are A TALE OF THREE KINGS by Gene Edwards and GOD'S SECRET TO GREATNESS by Dave Cape and Tommy Tenney.

Postcard from South Africa

Never thought I'd enjoy Christmas in the summer, but it's great in a kind of quirky way! The turkey was roasted on Christmas Eve and we had it cold with a salad buffet on Christmas Day – how weird is that? We sit outside under the stars talking till late most nights. It's the night sky that reminds me I am in Africa... It's great to be back. Missing Lucy though!
                    Claire

To: Kate

Subject: The Barclays

Hey you! How is it all going? Jon and Carol have just left, they came round for a meal with little Josie and were asking after all your news. I gave them a copy of your latest newsletter as they hadn't received it yet. Anyway, just thought I'd drop you a quick email before going to bed. It's been such a lovely day. Spring is in full swing now, the woods are looking beautiful with all the trees in full foliage. Lucy had a great time chasing rabbits this morning! I love it now the days are longer and the sun is warming up! My owl has been back now for a few weeks, yey! What's it like where you are? I guess there must be lots of preparations in the villages and towns for the Easter festivities. How are things with the team? Who was the one you were having a hard time with? I hope things are settling down.
Well, know that you are loved, much thought of, missed and prayed for.
Good night!
Claire

To: Kate

Subject: Team stuff

I hope you're feeling better! That episode with the fresh salad didn't turn out so good, hey? I am glad you were being looked after, but it's miserable being ill and away from home. I've been praying for you.

Sorry it's taken me a couple of days to reply to your last email, the server's been down – for a change! Hmmm… things sound a tad tense between you and Paul! I'm sorry it's stressing you out so much. It's frustrating how things like this can take up so much of our time and energy in sleepless nights and anxiety. I guess I just want to encourage you to hang in there. Don't give up on him. Apart from anything else, you need to work well together and to do that you need to have a good relationship with each other; it's about loving like Jesus showed us how.

> Do your part to live in peace with everyone, as much as possible.
>
> *Romans 12:18*

For me, learning to deal with conflict has been as tricky and freeing as learning to use and be under authority. The problem is that most of us never really learn to deal with it and so we find ourselves reliving similar conflicts over and over again in different situations with new people each time. There was one time I had a 'few issues' with one of my colleagues. It was funny, really. I was all ready to go in, guns blazing, and tell her all that was wrong with her and the way she did pretty much everything. And then, much to my annoyance, meetings got cancelled and routines were inexplicably changed. Meanwhile, in a moment of relative sanity, I pulled out my management notes and found some stuff on conflict under 'interpersonal skills in the workplace' – something I thought my colleague could do with getting her head around. I began reading and it was two weeks later that the two of us finally sat together for a private chat. The transformation that had taken place in me during those two weeks was astounding; there wasn't a gun in sight and we both left the meeting with our hearts none the worse for having been in each other's company. Through that episode I learnt that the most important thing in resolving conflict is restoring relationship, and that the major cause of any conflict may, in fact, be within ourselves.

> A gentle answer turns away wrath, but harsh words stir up anger.
>
> *Proverbs 15:1*

I also realised through that experience that often when things have gone wrong in a friendship or any working relationship, it's because of a combination of two things. Firstly, there is often a huge gap between the way I come across and how I intend to (and this was certainly true for my colleague). Secondly, the other person just happens to be pressing a series of 'wrong buttons' in me and actually it may be that God wants to deal with those things. At that time there were all sorts of insecurities and frustrations that were being triggered by the situation which God wanted me to address. I started out thinking that my colleague was the one in the wrong but then I saw that there was a lot in me that needed straightening out too.

Do you think there is anything about you that Paul needs to know so that he understands you better? What buttons is he pressing in you? Could you be coming across in a way that is hindering your friendship?

I hope this is helpful.

Let me know.

Claire

PS Drink lots of water (bottled!!)

To: Kate

Subject: re: re: Team stuff

***** Happy Easter ******

Morning!! Really glad it was a short-lived setback – it's

never a good thing to puke for long! I'm sure the rest did you good.

I totally understand that there are some things that need to change on his part. The thing is, as you deal with the stuff that I shared in my last email you'll be in better shape to give Paul constructive feedback. If I had given my colleague feedback before the two weeks were up, my motives would have been focused on my own need for revenge for the hurt, anger and frustration that I was feeling. After working through all that stuff, my motives were to restore a loving healthy relationship and to help her see how she was coming across so that she could change her behaviour and actions. Whenever I give feedback now, I try and make sure that I am doing so for the genuine good of the other person, out of love for them and the desire to see them grow. Does that make sense? The more love and acceptance you can sincerely communicate to the person you are giving feedback to, the more likely they are to be able to hear you and respond and change.

> Love is patient and kind. Love is not jealous or boastful or proud or rude. Love does not demand its own way.
> *1 Corinthians 13:4,5*

It excites me to think that God is going to use this situation to bring about significant growth in both you and Paul. I really encourage you to work through some of this stuff, choose to forgive so that God can begin to heal. There may be stuff that you need to ask God to forgive you for; as you do, pray for Paul. When you are ready to address some of the issues you want to with him from a motive of love, then here are some things that I have found helpful:
- Be careful not to abdicate responsibility for your feelings (none of the old 'you make me feel... ').
- Be careful to listen properly to everything he has to say.
- Be specific.

- Be truthful (don't exaggerate!).
- With the stuff he needs to change, discuss with him what changes might be helpful.
- In your timing, the environment you chose, the way you go about this: do your very best to communicate that you value and love him as a human being made in the image of God himself.

Did you notice that you started off feeling a little victimised but you are now taking responsibility for the situation, for your personal growth and for caring for Paul? Amazing!
Look, I know this stuff is really hard and it hurts to high heaven sometimes ... but be brave.
With all my love,
Claire

PS Stay away from the dodgy food stores!!
PPS Here are a few verses that I have been thinking through recently and trying to find ways of applying in my life. Maybe you could do some journalling on them too:
Romans 12:10,16–19
Matthew 5:43–48;6:14,15;7:1–5
John 13:34,35

Welcome home card

Welcome home!! Great to have you back! Make yourself totally at home here, help yourself to anything you need. I have set aside Wednesday and Saturday night in my diary so we can talk and pray through anything you want. Here's a rundown of what's on at the cinema and otherwise in town over the next couple of weeks and also a list of people's phone numbers so you can get in touch when you feel ready. There's a little basket of toiletries and other goodies put together by some of us who've been hanging on for you to get back – we hope it would help the re-adjustment process. Welcome home, my friend. Love Claire and Lucy-Lou

Year Five
Singleness/ Security

December 20th

Dear Kate

How are you, my friend? It sounds as though your new job is going really well. It is a good thing to feel stretched and I, for one, really appreciate feeling that there is plenty of room to grow. There are few things worse than walking all day in shoes that are too small for you; for me being in a job that doesn't allow me to grow is just like that.

Great to hear that you'll be around for mulled wine at my place on the 26th. I'm hoping Alex will be up from Brighton and Vicki should be there with Mavey too. It should be a lovely night with people coming and going through the evening. Christmas can be so much fun!

There was something you mentioned in one of your letters recently that's made me do a lot of thinking and that's what I am writing about. It's about the messages we (the church) send out about marriage and singleness. I have come to the conclusion (and I'd love to know what you think) that these messages are not all together helpful when it comes to setting priorities and ordering our lives in a God-honouring way.

> And the Lord God said, 'It is not good for the man to be alone. I will make a companion who will help him.'
> *Genesis 2:18*

I can see that much of what goes on around us and some of what is said implies that one of the ultimate goals of human existence and therefore God's purpose for each of us must be that we get married and have kids. I know that many people (including myself), perhaps the majority even, would like to marry and maybe have a family – that is a perfectly natural and God-created desire. My question is, can we assume that this desire will be granted on the basis of it being natural and God-given?

I know that God created man and woman and it wasn't good for them to be alone and I know he told them to multiply. I know that a fruitful, healthy marriage relationship is a wonderful picture of the unity of the Godhead and of our relationship with God. But I still don't think we can assume that this means that we all should and will be married. At a superficial level the maths doesn't work – at a much deeper level the longings that are often underlying our desire for marriage are not necessarily fulfilled in marriage.

Another thing that is often implied is that in order to be fully useful in God's church and complete in his presence, as well as attaining to his full purpose for us, we must be married. I have taken part in numerous conversations about criteria for filling positions in churches and church organisations where couples were preferred to a single person – not on the basis of who they were but purely on the fact that they were married.

Something I used to do, and I have heard countless others do the same, is choosing to put off some of the things that God has laid on your heart to do until after you are married. If we're talking about having kids,

then fair enough! Otherwise, I am not so sure...
especially if there's no fiancé around! I guess it's not
really surprising with all the messages we get from
the church about singleness and marriage, but I get so
frustrated when I see people putting parts of their lives
on hold because of it. Do you think you have been
affected by this, Kate? Whatever! Don't put off
answering God's call on your life because the truth is
we don't know what the future holds. There came a
point in my life when it no longer made sense to
make God's agenda for my life dependent on my
own agenda.

> ... some choose not to marry for the sake
> of the Kingdom of Heaven. Let anyone
> who can, accept this statement.
> *Matthew 19:12*

On my journey with this I have decided to be true
to what God has given me for today; the dreams, the
visions, the words. I would encourage anyone to do the
same. Walk with Jesus in the now; he holds your
future in his hands and he will meet you there.
Someone once helped me out in this dilemma by
describing a man and a woman as on two different
paths, and unbeknown to either of them their paths
converged in the distance. The idea is that they should
both get to the junction where their roads cross at the
same time, but if one of them stops on their journey
before the junction, that won't happen.

The point is, we don't know what lies ahead so
we need to keep in step with what God is saying to
us and calling us to now. Every journey is made up
of lots of steps without which you can't reach the

final destination.

If I could change the messages that we send out about singleness and marriage, this is what I would communicate: singleness is a gift and a privilege, as are marriage and parenthood; none of them is a right and they are never a curse. Each state is of equal value and delight to God. None of them comes with a guarantee for success or happiness. (The loneliest people I know are all married.) Making the single-life a God-life is a daily choice. Keeping a marriage alive and godly is a daily choice. Living the God-life as a parent is a daily choice. None of this happens automatically; but if you prayerfully work at it, God is faithful and we will see it begin to happen.

And this is what I would want to communicate to those who are single like me: for today you have the gift of singleness. You don't know how long you will have it. Be happy in it today, cherish it today, use it to honour Jesus and hold it lightly so that if the time should come to let it go you will be able to.

> … we are not all the same. God gives some the gift of marriage, and to others he gives the gift of singleness.
>
> *1 Corinthians 7:7*

Here's the maths bit. In the British church, single women outnumber single men by more than two to one! Most of the women like you and me are formed with the potential and God-given desire to marry and raise a family; but if part of living the God-life means that in choosing our marriage partner we must find someone who will wholeheartedly live the God-life

with us – in other words, a Christian – could it be that
at least half the single women in the church will have
to make a choice between marriage and the God-life?
And if we do choose our love for Jesus over our desire
to be married, how does that make God feel, I
wonder? I would guess that he is honoured and, like a
father is proud when his child makes a difficult but
right choice, so is he. Some say that if God wants you
to remain single he will take away the desire to be
married. I would say that's not always the case, but
instead it becomes a daily choice on our part to
honour God and serve him.

This is a very real issue for me and I find myself
coming back to it again and again and the ache
persists. I have put the closeness of my relationship
with God before my desire to be a wife and mother,
but the desire does not go away. I recognise the
longings that are behind my desire for marriage and I
have stopped asking for those longings to die because
they are an intrinsic part of who I am and who God
dreamed me to be; to kill them would be to lose a
part of my core.

Here's something else I have learnt: the deepest
longings of our hearts are infused with eternity and
echo God's intentions for us from ages past and future; they reach towards their fulfilment in eternity. I
long to be loved and protected but that will never
happen to the depth that I reach for in this life. No
human is able to give me that. But the fact that the
longing exists is hope that it will be fulfilled, that is
paradise. Meanwhile, 'though I know I will only be one
hundred per cent satisfied in Eden, until then, I am

happy with what is meant for me right now, knowing the best is yet to come. Writer John Eldredge (Journey of Desire) talks about this tension in terms of recognising our longings for the infinite and not trying to satisfy them with finite things.

> Our desire becomes insatiable because we've taken our longing for the infinite and placed it upon finite things.
>
> *John Eldredge*

One of my fears is that over the years we in the church have seen marriage as the most obvious solution to our need to be loved, protected and to know intimacy with another human heart. In the process we have lost sight of our need for community as Jesus intended. To an extent we have replaced community with marriage. One of the results is that those of us who stand alone are propelled towards marriage as the answer to our needs and those who are married find themselves still isolated. I believe we were made – marrieds and singles alike – for loving, self-giving community. For me, the answers to the desires that war in the deepest parts of who I am are found both in community and in eternity.

I have tried to share my heart with you on this. I am still on the journey and God is still working on me and teaching me. My prayer is that you would discover God's heart for you in this and in a new sense find your place in his heart again.

By the way, I have started getting the chiefs to think about the possibility of releasing me to go away for six months next year. If we plan well I think the youth ministry will grow and flourish – the team is strong enough to take it on and there are a couple of obvious choices for someone to hold the reins full-time while I am away. More to the point though, I really feel that I need some time out, some space to centre down and just be with God for a while. We will hopefully talk about it at my meeting with Phil and the others next week. I would really value your prayers about this. I just want to do what God wants, what's right for me and the youth ministry.

With all my love

Claire

April 10th

Dear Claire

I just wanted to write a short note to wish you all the best as you go on your travels. Thanks for always making me think and reminding me to keep my eyes on the finishing line. I am thankful for my life and the path that God has me on and I hope that, like you, I will be serving his purposes in all that I do. Thanks for inspiring me to love God and to live for him.

Have a great trip! Don't forget to come back someday soon…

All my love

Kate

Dear reader

As you've read my letters and emails to Kate you will have found some quotes from the Bible and from some favourite books that have shaped the ideas I have talked about. Here is an extra listing of Bible verses which have informed my thinking, and which I hope you will find useful to look at if you are wrestling with any of these issues yourself.

Discipleship

Isaiah 50:4	Luke 23:24	Matthew 28:18–20
Ephesians 5:1	Matthew 5:13–16	

Loneliness

John 14:16,17	John 20:22	Matthew 28:20
Hebrews 13:5	John 10:1	John 6:37
Romans 8:15–17	1 John 1:9	Matthew 13:44–46
Isaiah 43:4	Hebrews 4:14–16	John 14:30,31
Psalm 78:70–72	Exodus 2 – 3:1	Genesis 39 – 41
Luke 2:51,52	Matthew 4:1–11	

Temptation

Romans 7:18–20	2 Corinthians 3:18	Philippians 2:13
Galatians 2:8–10	Galatians 5:25	Psalm 32:5–9
James 1:4–15	Psalm 139:23,24	Hebrews 13:4
Hebrews 12:1	Galatians 6:1–3	James 5:16

Giving

Romans 12:4,5	1 Peter 5:1–4	Romans 6:15
Genesis 14:19,20	Matthew 5:17,27,28	Philippians 4:10,14–18
James 2:14–16	Acts 4:32-35	Luke 21:1–4
Romans 12:10–13	John 15:10	Matthew 6:24,33,34

Burnout

Romans 8:28	Jude 24	Mark 7:20
1 Timothy 4:7,8	Luke 6:12	John 6:11–20
Romans 12:6	2 Timothy 2:4–7	Psalm 37:34

Guidance

Deuteronomy 17:6	Philippians 4:6,7	1 John 2:27
Acts 16:6–12	Hebrews 4:12	Ephesians 5:18,19
Acts 12:25 – 13:3	Psalm 119:105	Psalm 25:14
John 5:15	John 10:27–29	Jeremiah 1:5
Ephesians 1:3–6	1 Corinthians 2:16	Proverbs 11:14
Proverbs 27:5,6,9,10,17	Isaiah 30:20,21	Psalm 27:14
Acts 17:26–28	Psalm 32:8,9	Psalm 37:23

Blessings and poverty

Psalm 139:1–12	Isaiah 40:21–26	Psalm 24:1
Luke 9:23,57–62	Ecclesiastes 3:1–8	Galatians 6:2
John 15:12	Psalms 17:7,8	Ecclesiastes 7:18 (NIV)
1 John 3:1,2	Galatians 2:20	Romans 8:16
Philippians 2:6,7,8	John 17:6–8	Luke 7:34
John 13:13–16	Matthew 6:4,6–18	

Authority

Matthew 20:25–28	Matthew 8:5–13	Hebrews 13:17
1 Peter 5:5,6	Luke 9:15–17	Galatians 6:4,5

Conflict

Romans 12:18	Matthew 7:1–5	Matthew 5:21–26
Matthew 18:21,22	Matthew 22:37–40	

Singleness

Genesis 2:18	Genesis 1:26–28	James 4:17
1 Corinthians 12:18	Ecclesiastes 3:11	

love
Claire

If you'd like to dialogue with Claire on any of the issues raised in this book, you can email her at letterstokate1@yahoo.com

Oriel's Diary

An Archangel's Account of the Life of Jesus

The personal diary of Archangel Oriel, colleague of Gabriel and Michael, records the birth, life, death and resurrection of Jesus Christ. Oriel takes up his pen in Heaven's administration department, as his Boss's plan to rescue humanity swings into action...

'… the life and times of Jesus … as you've never seen it recorded before … a skilful weaving of biblical fact and creative imagination … compelling insight into the man Jesus might have been'
Christianity & Renewal

Oriel's Travels

An Archangel's Travels with St Paul

From fanatical destroyer of the followers of Jesus to fearless gospel pioneer – Oriel tells the incredible story of Paul, the man central to the formation of the Church. Oriel's mission appears simple – to make sure one man gets to Rome, taking the Good News about Christ into the heart of the non-Jewish world. But his task is hindered by internal disagreements and external plots, forced flights and hair-raising escapes, shipwreck and imprisonment.

'… follows the Archangel Oriel as he guides St Paul's life … gripping reading … engagingly written … a real page-turner' **Baptist Times**

Oriel in the Desert
An Archangel's Account of the Life of Moses

What does it take to transform an unbelieving melancholic murderer into the godly leader of a new nation? Oriel gives us an inside track on Moses, who rises from a dysfunctional family background to engage in the intrigue of Egyptian politics. After head-to-head confrontation with his step-cousin Pharaoh Rameses II, Moses leads the escape from forced labour of the demoralised slaves who are destined to become God's chosen people.

A trilogy from Robert Harrison, published by **Scripture Union.**

Dear Bob
by Annie Porthouse

Dear Bob,
Thought would write you, my future husband, diary re uni life. V much looking forward to meeting you. Prob you are super – Cn (Cliff Richard?) and hot bloke (maybe not…) and like Pringles, tiramisu, marriage…

Jude Singleton is about to face the biggest challenge of her life – she is looking for a man! On the way to finding 'Bob' she has to deal with those annoying distractions of university life: broken toes, waterproof curtains and driving instructors with dubious breath. Oh, and she's not sure whether there is a God, after all…

Love Jude
by Annie Porthouse

Having survived her first year of uni, Jude Singleton has resolved some of her earlier spiritual difficulties. But will she be able to keep it all together when she finds a boyfriend?

The sequel continues Annie Porthouse's realistic look at student life and culture. Hilarious!

Dear Bob, Love Jude and the Oriel trilogy are published by Scripture Union. To order:

- phone SU's mail order line: 01908 856006
- email info@scriptureunion.org.uk
- fax 01908 856020
- log on to www.scriptureunion.org.uk
- write to SU Mail Order, PO Box 5148, Milton Keynes MLO, MK2 2YX